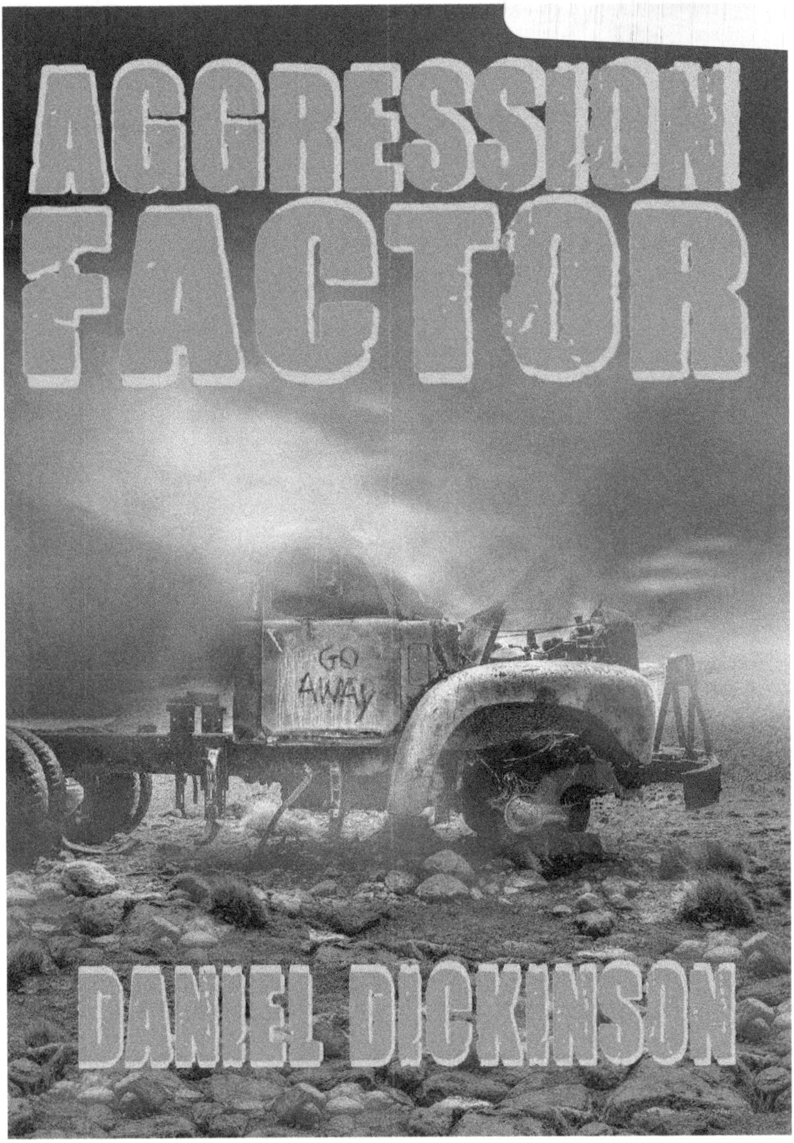
AGGRESSION
FACTOR
GO AWAY
DANIEL DICKINSON

Aggression Factor

By Daniel Dickinson

DEDICATION

This book is dedicated to my daughter. Thank you for being the best child anyone could ever ask for. I loved you since the first moment I held you in my arms. You're my best friend. As I watched you grow to be the woman you've become, I hoped and prayed (you know praying isn't my thing) that I gave you all the tools you'd need to not only survive but grow with. At the same time, it was hard to watch you do your own thing and to give you the space you needed to become who you are. I hope that I was able to provide you with wisdom and knowledge, to be the best version of yourself you could be. I just hope you know how much you mean to me. I gave everything I could and hope enough of it stuck. Because whether you know it or not, learning is always going to be part of the journey, and don't wait. Be hungry to learn more, experience things, see things, and meet new people. You need to experience everything. Because it's what makes you, you. Thank you for putting up with me. Thank you for being my best friend. I love you daughter.

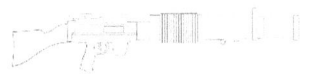

1

FALLEN IRON

Oh! I have slipped the surly bonds of Earth
And danced the skies on laughter-silvered wings;
Sunward I've climbed, and joined the tumbling mirth
of sun-split clouds,-and done a hundred things
You have not dreamed of-wheeled and soared and swung
High in the sunlit silence. - "High Flight" by John G.
Magee

ir rushed through his blond hair, whipping the strands into a frenzy like corn stalks in a tornado. A smile as large as the bright blue sky plastered his face.

"Hang on!" his dad called needlessly over the howl of the biplane's large engine.

Laughter escaped Mike's lips as his dad rolled the plane's bright yellow wings. It was as if the world had been turned upside down by the hand of some child's fancy.

"The Horde landed outside of New Washington. They have already pushed east toward the Potomac from Annandale. We need every available armor unit out on the front lines. We are the last line of defense, boys," General Mactavish growled. "The line in the sand is the Potomac. They cannot cross it! Do I make myself clear?"

"Yes, sir!" The room erupted.

"Then get out there!" he said.

The room of pilots dispersed. Many of them were new, younger airmen who hadn't seen combat. Mike stood among them, gathering his notes and preflight plan. He peered sidelong at his wing, a group of men slightly older than his own forty years of age.

"You scared?" he asked his wingman Friday.

She glanced up from her own notes and then stood, gathering them up. "Nope, you?"

"Shitless." he smiled.

"Hey, flyboys, we'll clean up this mess. Don't you worry your feathered faces about it," a pilot Mike knew as Heath chided.

The Kid, which is what Mike referred to him as carried himself with confidence. He was top of his class and had more simulated kills than anyone else here.

Mike's wingman growled and stomped toward Heath, but Mike put a hand on her shoulder. "It's not worth it."

The rest of Mike's unit gathered around them, clearly irritated by Heath's inflammatory words.

"Yeah, you had your chance, old man. The Air Force couldn't stop the invasion. Don't worry, we'll mop them up for you." Heath grinned.

"The Marines must be lying about if they're calling us in." One of the other pilots chuckled.

Heath laughed. "Maybe they got distracted with all the pretty colors."

"Is there a problem here?" General Mactavish snapped as he approached the group of men.

Mike and the rest of the pilots snapped to attention. "No, sir!"

"Good. I need all the men on the front line. That includes you." Mactavish looked at each man in turn, "Is that understood? Report to your units now!"

"Yes, sir!" The men replied and headed to the hanger.

Heath pushed past Mike and Friday, and the rest of the winged unit.

"We did what we could, didn't we?" Friday asked. She watched the younger pilots disappear around the corner with cold blue eyes.

Mike peered over his shoulder to see the rest of the men he had flown with during the invasion. The first few hours, when the battle had taken place in the skies above, were brutal. The US Airforce did its best against the faster, sleek invaders. It was a shock to their sense of superior air power.

On the ground, the army was woefully outgunned when lumbering alien mechs stomped across the country toward their positions. Firing large shells that landed with thunderous explosions, wiping out tanks and men alike.

He sighed heavily, remembering all the losses they had sustained then. So many men and women died that morning. The Horde had pushed east after invading the heartland several weeks ago. It was theorized that they had met unexpected resistance in the West and turned their attention to the East.

That was beyond Mike's pay grade, however. He turned his attention back to Friday. "We did all we could."

"They don't think so," Friday said with a thrust of her chin toward the eager pilots.

Mike shrugged. "They're young. What do they know about living and dying?"

The group of pilots rounded the corner and entered the hangar where newly built power armor was being energized and staged for deployment.

"I hate those things," Friday whispered.

Mike completed his startup, and the aircraft hummed around him. He glanced at the power armor and shook his head. He hated those things just as much as Friday did. They were bulky, slow, and easy targets for faster foot soldiers.

He and his squadron were one of only a dozen air support wings left, and to compound the issue, there were not enough pilots in the fleet to man all of the aircraft. The candidates that were still in service were assigned to pilot the new power armor. The armor was a hybrid of flying and ground assault weaponry that resembled a video game character more than the pinnacle of military might.

Mike was given the opportunity to learn the new system, but because it was designed and built around stolen Horde tech, he wanted nothing to do with it. Instead, like Friday and the rest of his squadron of aging A-10g pilots, he chose to stay with his old friend, the 'Warthog.'

"You old geezers ready for this? You replace the batteries in your pacemaker?" Heath said over the intercom.

"Pipe down Alpha-1, get your team into position for launch. Iron-1, all systems show green. You are clear to taxi runway 19, right," The commander's voice called from the speaker in his helmet.

"Alpha-1, ready for launch," Heath's voice said over the coms.

Mike watched as the bulky, vaguely man-shaped armor was launched, the temporary wings and jet pack vibrating against the mech from the strain of being pushed through the air. His eyes returned to the taxiway as he maneuvered his A-10g "Warthog" around to the runway. He looked out of the oval glass cockpit to see Friday and the rest of his wing were close behind.

"Iron-1, standby for go," the commander said.

An explosion erupted nearby, muted and barely audible through the canopy of his aircraft.

"Wha-" Mike was cut off as Heath broke in over coms.

"The Horde, they are everywhere!" Heath said.

"Alpha-1, regroup with Charlie Echo 11, provide support, and keep the chatter down," the commander replied.

There was another explosion, closer than the last, and it shook the ground.

"Iron-1, you are clear for takeoff. Come to heading two seven zero, and climb to flight level three zero and commence," the commander said over the radio.

"Copy. Heading two seven zero, and climb to flight level three zero," Mike said with practiced precision.

There was another explosion, this one from the engines, as Mike pushed forward on the throttle. The aircraft rolled forward, slowly at first. His heartbeat pounded harder in anticipation of the growing speed. Adrenaline coursed through his veins, not from fear. But from the freedom flying gave him.

Pressure built against his chest as he pulled back on the stick, pushing him into the seat. Mike banked the aircraft right and glanced back to see the last of his wing make it off the ground before an explosion erupted at the base gates.

"Godspeed, Iron-1," his commander said over the com as gunshots echoed in the background.

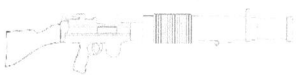

Mike checked the gauges. Everything appeared in order. To this day, the upper brass debated the need for the aged aircraft and whether it could be replaced. To Mike, however, there was no question of its continuous need on the battlefield. He considered them Angels, and he felt a close affinity for them. Far greater than any new, shiny technology, like the power armor.

"Echo Charlie 11 actual, this is Iron-1 ready for tasking," Mike said over the intercom as he leveled the plane's wings out.

"Iron-1, this is Echo Charlie 11 actual, glad to see your birds made it in the air," the voice on the ground said through broken static. "The Horde has artillery in the southwest, bearing two three two. See if you can't take the pressure off us. And be careful; we've seen a Buzzard up there."

"Copy that. Artillery bearing two three two. We'll be careful. Iron-1 out," Mike replied and then switched his coms to the squadron. "Alrighty, boys and girls, you heard the man, set up for an attack run. Let's find that artillery and take it out. Iron-4 and Iron-5, climb to flight level five zero. Keep an eye out for that Buzzard."

Mike sighed internally. A Buzzard. Great. We're not dogfighters; we'll be torn to shreds.

Mike led Friday and Iron-3 toward the artillery and scanned the horizon for the target. They were easy to spot among the ruined cityscape below them.

Destroyed buildings and uncontrolled fire razed what was once Alexandria. Large circular entrenchments with at least a half dozen Horde mechs surrounded the gun placement.

A plume of smoke rose from the tops of the artillery as they rained shells down on the marines and power armor several miles east.

"Alright, Iron-3, laze that emplacement and get a missile on target," Mike said, "Iron-2 and I will provide backup."

"Copy that. Target lit and ready to fire in 3... 2—" Iron-3 didn't finish the count as his plane exploded in a ball of flame.

13

"Iron-4 to Iron-1, Buzzard at your 5 high! Bank, bank, bank!" Iron-5 yelled into the coms. His muscles had already yanked hard right on the first warning.

Loud thunder echoed through the thick glass of the canopy, and he saw the black Buzzard speed past.

Training took over, and Mike prepared his plane for close air combat with no illusions of whether he was about to die. His aircraft was meant for low and fast strikes barely above the treetops. The Buzzard was built by the Horde for fast, air-to-air combat. It was sleek, black, and hummed with energy.

Mike frantically looked out the canopy, trying to spot the black wings of death as they circled above them. He didn't see it.

"Iron-4, Iron-5, do you have it?" Mike asked, "Iron 2, Friday, get that artillery lazed, I'll— There, bank left! Iron-2, bank left!"

His warning came too late, however, as Friday's A-10g lost a wing, then exploded in flame.

"No!" Mike yelled, "Goddamnit! Friday!"

Red-hot anger narrowed his vision to pinpricks; the only thing he saw was the shadow of the aircraft that just killed his closest friend.

"Iron-4 and Iron-5, I need you to start your attack run on the artillery. Go low and fast," Mike said through clenched teeth. He was setting up the others as bait, his stomach roiled in anguish and remorse. It was his job to see the squadron was safe, and he had failed. Now he was taking a risk on luring the Buzzard out in the open. The alien vessel was fast, but it was not maneuverable at low altitudes.

Mike pulled back on the stick and leveled out above Iron-4 and Iron-5. There was no sign of the Buzzard. His anger burned deeper. "Where are you?" he growled. "Iron-4 and 5, laze the target and fire as soon as you have tone."

"Copy," they said one after another.

14

The Buzzard darted from the clouds above. Mike saw the dark blur of its visage from the corner of his eye. He yanked hard right and banked away from it. The Buzzard was faster than his slow ground assault aircraft. But what he lacked in speed, he made up for in low-altitude maneuverability.

"I got—" he was cut off as the Buzzard fired its laser cannon at the two A-10s below them. "Iron-4, look out!"

Iron-4 exploded as the red-hot laser rounds penetrated the fuselage of the aircraft.

"Missile's away!" Iron-5 shouted seconds before being shot from the sky. Twin smoke trails dropped to the ground nearly side by side as both aircraft crashed to the earth.

Mike circled around behind the Buzzard and fired his only two missiles at the aircraft. They snaked through the blue sky toward the alien craft. The Buzzard pulled up as the missiles exploded underneath, missing it completely.

"Fuck," Mike mumbled as the Buzzard turned its attention to him.

Mike knew the only thing he could do now was to stay behind him. He rolled his aircraft and dove toward the wreckage of the artillery and the burned-out shells of the buildings.

"Let's see you follow me down here," he growled. He heard the uneasy sounds of small arms fire hitting the aircraft, but he paid little mind to them.

The Buzzard turned and threatened Mike in a high-stakes game of chicken. Mike smiled. The Buzzard was faster and more maneuverable at high altitudes, but down here, the A-10 ruled. If that wasn't enough of an edge, the Buzzard made a fatal mistake. He exposed himself to the very thing that made the A-10 what it was.

With a yell of rage, Mike pulled the trigger on the stick, firing at the Buzzard. Lasers flew past him while some of the rounds burst through the titanium plate that surrounded the cockpit, sending smoke and shrapnel spiraling through the glass and out the other side. With the familiar smell of gunpowder and a rumbling that shook the entire core of the A-10, the Buzzard ran into the stream of lead that Mike had fired at him.

Mike's pull of the trigger shredded the thin shadow skin of the Buzzard, sending chunks of it flying as the speed of the aircraft worked against it. The Buzzard tried to correct its course and move away from the hail of bullets, but it was already too late. The gatling of the A-10 had torn the craft in two.

Mike laughed triumphantly, and he pulled up away from the Buzzard's carcass as it ripped apart and fell to the earth.

"I got the bastard, Friday. I got him," he said, peering down at the burning wreck. As his eyes moved back toward his cockpit, he took stock of what occurred and saw several holes through the aircraft. The thick titanium tub-like cockpit he sat in protected him from most of the laser's fierceness.

Shards of searing metal embedded themselves in his leg following the explosion, causing his jumpsuit to be soaked in profuse bleeding. As the initial surge of adrenaline faded, waves of pain washed over him, prompting involuntary winces.

Mike pushed the button to his mic, "Iron-1 to Echo Charlie 11 actual."

"Go ahead, Iron-1," the voice on the other end replied.

"The artillery is down. Iron-1 on station for tasking," he said through the pain of pushing the rudders in with his feet, the blood seeping into his boot.

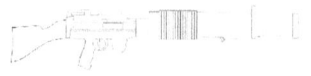

16

Mike heard Echo Charlie 11, but he also heard the wind whistling through the holes in the cockpit. He lifted his nose to inhale the fresh air, and his spirit lifted once again as he recalled his childhood flying with his father. The laughter as they flew seemingly recklessly through the air. The only thing between them and gravity was the power and majesty of the biplane they were flying.

His thoughts were interrupted by the sound of bullets ricocheting off the wings from the small arms fire below. The Horde is desperately shooting at me, he thought offhandedly.

"Echo Charlie 11 actual to Iron-1, I repeat, there is an anti-aircraft battery heading two eight zero. Alpha-1 is engaged but has not responded," the voice said over the comms.

"Copy that. I'll take a look," Mike replied, glanced down at his legs, they were growing cold, and he was feeling sleepy.

Mike turned the aircraft painfully in the direction Echo Charlie indicated and gained a few feet in altitude in order to have a better position for any type of attack run he might need to employ. Assuming, of course, I don't get shot out of the sky first.

"Iron-1 to Alpha-1, come in," Mike said over the comms.

"Alpha... Danger... Anti—" came a staticky and broken reply.

"Say again, Alpha-1."

There was no response.

Mike looked out over the battlefield and saw a group of power armor desperately holding the Horde back from the anti-aircraft battery. The guns turned toward him, and fire erupted in succession as the air around his cockpit exploded.

Mike pushed down and tried to keep the trees and other broken buildings between him and the cannons, but it was no use. Part of his wing was missing, and he knew he would have a harder time maneuvering.

"Alpha-1, clear your men from the battery," Mike called over the radio.

"Old man, is that you?" Heath said, with a grunt, "Retreat isn't in my vocabulary."

Mike sighed and banked toward the battery. Climbing again, he aimed his own gatling gun toward the line of Horde attackers that surrounded Heath and the rest of his unit.

"Suit yourself, but I'm bringing the rain; you may want to back up," Mike said.

"Wai—"Heath was cut off as Mike pulled the trigger and let loose a stream of lead toward the Horde and the anti-aircraft cannon. As he did, the battery fired several rounds, exploding against the fuselage.

Mike pulled the aircraft up and away from the smoldering ruins, causing pain to wash over him in a wave of nausea. The nose of the aircraft pointed up toward the sky, and he couldn't see the ground. Blue sky and white clouds, like welcoming pillows, beckoned him.

"Not yet," he whispered and pushed down once again toward the front line and the line of power armor.

The Horde had recovered from Mike's last attack run, and now, with the anti-aircraft cannon nearly destroyed, they were focused completely on Heath and the rest of his unit.

"Now you pissed them off," Heath said, explosions and rifle fire punctuating his words.

Mike ignored him, and he dove his A-10 toward the Horde. The anti-aircraft cannon came around and focused its barrels on him.

Mike glanced up and saw the explosions from the anti-aircraft cannon but smiled and pushed the button near his thumb. He pulled up and threw the last bomb he had at the Horde, who were re-enforcing the front line.

Pain and burning sensation warmed him. He realized too late that there was a fire burning near his legs. He felt none of it. All he could feel was... freedom.

His eyes were focused on the blue sky and those welcoming clouds. He laughed gleefully as if he were a kid again. Tears of relief streamed down his face in warm rivulets.

"Alpha-1 to Iron-1, ground units are secure; you are clear for return tasking," Heath's voice said over the coms.

Mike knew it was too late. He was cold, despite the fire that was burning near his legs. He was sleepy and content. His face was, after all, pointed toward the heavens and the bright blue glory he came to love as a child.

"Alpha-1 to Iron-1, Mike? You hear me, you're smoking, head back to base," Heath said over coms.

Heath's words went unheard as Mike smiled and whispered, "I'm coming home, Dad."

The A-10 exploded in a streak of fire like a flaming arrow fired into the sky.

2

ELLIE

"A father is, to a daughter, like a warrior. He is her shield, her armor. He is her sword, her dagger. He is her Merlin, wizened with age and wisdom." -Unknown proverb

ake up, Ellie. We have to go." A voice echoed through her mind. Did it come from outside her dream, or maybe inside it? She could not tell.

"Wake up. Now." She opened her eyes at the increased urgency to see her father's bearded face peering down at her. Gentle green eyes watched her, agitation playing at the edge of his features.

She scanned the dingy, sparsely furnished room and noticed a dark bundle by the door.

"Wha-"

He cut her short. "Get up and get dressed quickly. Pack your go bag. We are leaving. Hurry!" Dawn crept through the broken window. Boards covering the windows let in spears of orange light that pierced the darkened room.

She did as instructed while he disappeared down the hall adjacent to her room. She could hear him rattling around the room beside hers, and when he came back, he wore what he called his traveling cloak. It was more of a duster with a hood than the fictional cloak she had read about in fantasy stories.

"Come on! The Horde is coming," he said, more urgently than before.

This got Ellie moving faster. She wore her ratty pants, boots, shirt, and leather vest. Before running out of the bedroom, she tossed her brown hair back and tied it up.

He stood by the front door, his bag slung over his shoulders. He had his sword and Ellie's bow and quiver in one hand. A pistol hung at his hip in a roughed-up leather holster. It was a Black .45 caliber that held twelve rounds and one in the chamber. Like the rest of the weaponry in his hands, it was well taken care of.

"Those won't work against them. You know that," she said, furrowing her brow.

He shook his head. "These are not for them. We're not staying."

The world was not a safe place.

There was an explosion in the near distance, and she jumped.

He thrust the bow and quiver at her so hard that she gasped. "Let's go!" He pushed open the board that had served as a door and set out into the rising sun.

They ran down the street, away from the direction of the explosion. Keeping to the burnt-out husks of buildings and vehicles, they used what cover they could find.

After a mile, he slowed his pace. Ellie's chest burned from the exertion. She hated running.

"Wh-why... Why are they attacking? It's been-"

"Sixteen years," he said softly. "I know." His expression, fleeting as it was, almost seemed like sorrow.

Ellie started to ask why he was looking at her like that, but another explosion spurred them on.

"Come on. We have to find shelter," her father said.

They walked quickly away. With each step she took, Ellie knew they would never see her home again. Despite being winter, the combination of the sun's rays and the effort expended while trekking through the barren expanse of debris proved draining.

After a few hours of climbing through deserted and destroyed buildings, the Tunnels loomed from the concrete mounds of long-forgotten buildings. As they approached, they heard men shouting about their arrival.

"Stay close," her dad said.

She did not respond and only peered up at him. She wanted to say something back. A smart-ass response had come to mind, but as she opened her mouth to say it, he glanced down at her with a glower.

"Stop! Identify yourself!" a man from the gate called.

23

The Tunnels were old, leftovers from the world before it became overrun with the Horde. Giant metal gates, which once had been semi-trucks, guarded the entrance. She had never seen one of the eighteen-wheelers working. Those she had seen were only in magazines found in abandoned libraries.

"We're from the outskirts. We're looking for shelter," her dad called back.

"Fine, come in. You bring news of the east?" the gatekeeper asked.

"We do. The Horde attacked about 20 miles from here."

The man stopped pulling the chain to open the gate and peered down from his guard tower. "That-that's impossible. The Horde hasn't been seen around here in a long time. They don't like the desert."

"I don't bring lies to you," her father replied.

The man nodded and opened the gate faster. "Come on in and tell us everything."

"Stay close," her dad said, fixing her with a stern glare. "We're not staying long."

"What? Why?" Ellie said.

"The Horde won't be far behind us. Nowhere is safe out here in the wilds," he said as he adjusted his bag.

The gate slowly pulled aside on its metal track. The loud metal scraping echoed through the walled canyon that led to the Tunnels' entrance.

"Welcome to the Tunnels," a burly man with a torn cowboy hat said. "I'm Sheriff Mason. Keep your weapons holstered, and we'll have no troubles."

Ellie's dad nodded, "Of course."

"There's not a lot of room. If you can find a spot that isn't claimed, you can squat there for as long as you need," Sheriff Mason said.

"We'll be going shortly. Do you have food or water? I'll trade ammo."

The sheriff nodded. "Yessir, go see Mackellin over there, on your left. He'll have what you need."

"Thank you."

Ellie followed her dad and the sheriff through the gate to the darkened tunnels. Men, women, and children huddled quietly in the shadows of lean-tos, cobbled-together shacks, and overall filth. The smell of unwashed bodies mixed with human waste was overwhelming. Ellie glanced up at her father, but he showed no outward appearance of disapproval of the conditions. The humid, condensed air of too many people breathing in cramped quarters was stifling. Droplets trickled like bugs down her back.

They walked to the west end of The Tunnels and found a small space to rest.

"Wait here," her dad said, dropping his pack beside her. "Don't talk to anyone, and don't move."

She looked up at him. His black hair fell in front of his piercing eyes as if daring her to disobey.

"Why are you being so mean to me?" she asked as he pulled a box of ammo from the bag.

He scoffed at her. "I'm being firm. If you want me to be mean, I can. But more to your point, I know you."

Ellie glanced at him, dejected. "What does that mean?"

"It means," he said as he pulled another box out and put it in his pocket, "You'll wander off the first chance you get. You're more like me than you admit."

She rolled her brown eyes at him.

With a smile, he rose to his feet and disappeared down the tunnel to barter for food and water.

Ellie pulled her pack close to her and rummaged through it. They had left so quickly that she only had necessities: clothing, a sleeping bag, water canteen, and trail mix. It was only enough for a short, quick escape if needed. She never thought they would actually use it. She glanced down the tunnel where her father had disappeared into the crowd, thinking about what he taught her for packing her go bag. He had insisted she carry as much but as little as possible. Each extra ounce of weight would be felt more the further they walked. She checked the quiver attached to her bag. She had 12 broad head arrows. It would be enough to get them by for a while if she used them for hunting.

Hunting was not her favorite pastime. She thought of the last time her father took her out. They found a deer in the higher elevations of the valley. It had been grazing, and was unaware of their approach. Its ears twitched toward them as if it had sensed them, but it ignored the warnings. With a twang, an arrow flew and pierced the deer's side, burying the arrowhead deep in its heart. Blood pumped rhythmically from the wound as the heart spewed the last remaining drops onto the dirt. She hated the way it made her feel afterward. Regret; she hated it. She blamed her dad for the experience, and the remorse lingered for months afterward.

Sitting in the dank, filth-ridden Tunnels with only a small bag of trail mix, she realized she was starving. They had not eaten anything since dinner the night before, and, ironically, she would kill for some of her dad's deer stew now.

"Hello," a voice said, breaking her reverie. Ellie peered up to see a young man standing in front of her. Dust caked his pale skin and matted his light brown hair.

"Hello?" she replied before she knew what she was doing. She sighed inwardly. Her dad was going to have kittens if he found out she was talking to a stranger, especially if that person was a boy her age.

"My name is Marcus," the young man said, holding out a dirty hand.

She studied it awkwardly before accepting it. It was firm and rough from digging in the dirt, "Ellie."

"You're new here, huh?" Marcus said as he plopped down in front of her, crossing his legs as he sat.

"Yes," she said, fidgeting with the backpack's strap.

"Do you always speak in one-word answers?" Marcus asked with a grin.

"No," Ellie replied, then closed her eyes and giggled. "Sorry, I did it again."

Marcus chuckled. "It's okay. What brings you to The Tunnels?"

Ellie looked around to see if anyone was listening. "The Horde attacked a settlement near our home. East of here."

The boy's blue eyes shot wide open. "They're here? In the desert? I was told they didn't like it here. Too dry or something."

Ellie shrugged nervously. "Quiet down. You'll cause a panic," she said. Her dad's voice echoed in her head, but the words were her own.

Marcus grew quiet. "You're right. Sorry. Still, they haven't been here for some time. Why now?"

"I don't know. The last time they attacked was when I was a baby. That's when my mom..." She grew quiet, averting her eyes from his to hide her pain. She was not old enough to remember the traumatic event. However, her father had told her about it only once and only because she asked.

"Those invaders--they should have been killed a long time ago," Marcus said with a shake of his head.

"I heard they are invincible," Ellie said. "I don't think they can be killed. If so, wouldn't-"

"Can I help you?" a voice said from behind Marcus. The two teenagers glanced up to see Ellie's dad looming above them, jerky and a jug of water in his hands.

"Oh, sorry, sir, no. I was just leaving," Marcus said, scrambling to his feet. "It was nice meeting you, Ellie."

27

"You too," Ellie said with a smile before the boy scurried off down the tunnel lined with shacks.

"Who was that?" Ellie's father asked, packing the food in his bag.

"Marcus. Why'd you scare him off?" Ellie said indignantly.

Her dad glanced up at her with an arched brow. "I didn't do anything. I just asked if I could help him."

"As if you did so out of the kindness of your heart," she said with a glower that almost mirrored his own. "I'm not your baby anymore."

He sighed and sat beside her, leaning against the tunnel wall. "No, you're not. You've had to grow up faster than any child should." They sat in uncomfortable silence for a minute before he said anything more. "The Tunnels have been made aware of the Horde. People say that eastern border refugees have taken shelter in Old Vegas. That's where we're going. You'll be safe there."

"Th-that's a long way away. And through marauder lands. Why can't we fight? Didn't you beat them once before?"

Ellie's dad shook his head slowly. "No. The only thing that kept the Horde at bay was their hatred for the desert conditions. Maybe they are here now because it's cooler? Maybe because it's been a wetter season than normal? Who can say? But it's not safe anymore."

"What about these people?" Ellie asked.

Her dad sighed. "Get some rest while you can, Ellie. We're leaving in a few hours." He closed his eyes, ending any further conversation.

Ellie looked at him with contempt. *How can he be so callous?* she thought.

She sat back against her bag and closed her eyes but could not fall asleep. She found her mind traveling to Marcus. "He was cute," she thought, "and brave." He at least said something to her dad instead of scrambling off in fear.

When her dad took her to town, she didn't get much chance to interact with kids her age. The only time she did this was when she was in school. He would escort her there and home again like a stalwart guardian. She understood why, though. There were thieves and murderers all over the valley. She had no illusions that they lived in safety.

Still, she thought, we're safe here. I should be able to talk to people my age. I'm grown up; I don't need him anymore.

Her consciousness faded away after that. She didn't dream, just faded off into black slumber, the type of sleep that felt hard, fast, and unrestful.

There was an explosion somewhere nearby, causing everyone to jolt awake. Her father beside her was jumping to his feet. She heard him cursing himself for falling asleep. His eyes narrowed in anger--not at her, but at himself. He had lowered his guard.

Screams echoed through The Tunnels as men, women, and children cried in warning and terror.

"The Horde, they're here!" someone shouted in the distance.

"Run!" her dad yelled, throwing his backpack on. He grabbed his sword, a slightly curved blade with a talon for a pommel, and kept his other hand free.

She grabbed her gear and began to run toward the back exit of the tunnel. People were shoving and pushing, and she tried to keep up with her dad. A man and woman pushed between them, and she lost sight of her father for a second.

Chaos ignited around them as another explosion erupted behind her.

"Dad?!"

Screams were her only response. Panic bubbled up through her chest in a wave of nausea and fear.

She emerged from the other end of the tunnel into the darkening sky. The people began to spread out as she ran down the broken highway. She stopped and glanced around, straining to find her father, but he was nowhere in sight.

"Marcus!" she called. The boy she had met earlier ran past, and she darted after him.

He glanced at her, panic in his eyes. "They're killing everyone in the Tunnels! Run!"

She crested the hill nearby and could feel warm water dripping down her face: tears. She was scared.

Suddenly, in the growing darkness, several shapes bolted toward them. Marcus stumbled to a stop. Her knees suddenly felt like lead weights, and she came to a halt beside him.

The green-skinned creatures howled in triumph. One of them raised its rifle in the air as if trying to scare them in the other direction. Its grotesque face snarled as it approached the two children.

Ellie's instincts took over. She had to fight. Her dad's insistent drilling guided her hands as she notched an arrow and let it loose at the closest Horde creature. It found the meaty flesh of its eye and sunk in deep enough that the creature yelped once and then stumbled to the ground.

"Th-they are not indestructible," Marcus said, mouth agape.

We can fight them, Ellie realized distantly through the cloud of focused survival.

The other creature watched its dead comrade fall to the ground and howled in rage. Three more of the Horde joined him and then ran at the two children.

There was a loud bang, and one of the creatures fell to the ground at Ellie's feet. Her dad jumped in front of her, a flash of silver light trailed the swing of his sword, and another of the creatures fell to the earth. She tried to nock another arrow, but her hands were shaking. Another bang, and then the last one fell as the sword sank into its ribs.

"Run!" Her dad said.

She did as instructed and ran. Marcus was close behind. Her dad brought up the rear.

They ran west along the highway and then broke north through the ruined outskirts of town. It was not until she stumbled that they began to slow their pace. She looked over her shoulder at her dad, who had also slowed. He was panting heavily in large gulping breaths.

Ellie put the arrow she hadn't realized she still held back in the quiver. Her dad holstered his pistol and sheathed his sword. They stopped sometime later on the outskirts of the ruined cityscape. In the darkened distance, they saw a firelight flickering near the spot they knew as the Tunnels. The last safe haven in the valley was burning.

"Let's go," Ellie's dad said after a minute of rest. "We need to get into the hills before sunrise. They'll have a harder time finding us there."

"Marcus. Y-your family?" Ellie said.

He shook his head. "I lost them when I was eight."

"Oh. I-I'm sorry," Ellie said. "He can come with us, right, Dad?"

Her father looked Marcus over, then shrugged.

Ellie leaned toward Marcus. "That's as good of an answer as you'll get."

"Thank you, sir," Marcus said, holding out a hand to him.

Her dad took the offered hand begrudgingly and shook it. "Let's go."

The three of them marched through the night, the sporadic light of the stars and the moon lighting their way. Splintered and shattered from decades of disrepair, the broken roads guided them north into the highlands. They slept in small rotations. Her father took the first watch while Ellie and Marcus slept. When the sun rose, they continued on till noon. Then her dad slept for a few hours before moving further north.

"We stop here for the night," her dad said abruptly on the eve of the second night. They were in a gorge of sorts. Water ran from north to south in a shallow creek. "We are going to spend a full night here, resting. Tomorrow, we enter Marauder territory. We'll need our energy to get through there."

Marcus looked at Ellie nervously. "Marauders?"

"We'll be fine," Ellie's dad muttered, setting his bag down. He untied two rabbits they had caught early in the morning.

Ellie tossed her bag beside his and sat down in the dirt, where she began to make a circle of rocks. She hollowed out the center and stacked small sticks in the middle, like a tepee. She took out a worn piece of flint and her knife, then began scraping sparks into the small bundle of mesquite bark and dried grass. With a few attempts, she had a fire going. Another thing her dad had taught her, she realized.

She glanced toward her dad and saw he had dressed the rabbits and was skewering them with long branches. Smoke from the branches would add ample flavor. Her mouth watered at the thought. He knew exactly how to cook them, and the smell brought back good memories of the two of them camping in the north country when things were quieter.

Ellie scooted toward Marcus and smiled. "You ever had campfire smoked rabbit?"

"Nope," he said. "It looks amazing. Granted, I could eat dirt."

"Well, you don't need to do that," Ellie's father said with a grin as he stuck the ends of the rabbit skewers in the dirt. "Marcus, that water is fresh from the mountains. Can you fill our canteens?"

"Yes, sir," Marcus said as he stood. The young man grabbed all the water containers and took them down to the creek a few feet away.

Ellie studied her dad as he watched the boy leave. Then he looked at her, his gaze gentle but also pained. She didn't understand why.

He smiled at her. "You like him, don't you?"

Ellie's eyes flew open. "What?" She spluttered. "W-what?"

He chuckled. "Yeah, that's what I thought." He sat down across from her. His features seemed older to her somehow, haggard and drained. "I've seen you two huddled close, whispering. I see the looks you two give one another when the other is unaware."

"He gives me looks?"

Her dad chuckled. "Yes."

She beamed.

"I suppose this was only a matter of time. It's not something I can keep you from." Her father sighed as he picked up a branch and poked the fire. It crackled in protest. "I've taught you to read, hunt, trade. To survive."

"I know," she replied, fixing him quizzically. "What's that got to do with Marcus?"

He shrugged. "It's the one thing I haven't taught you. It's not something I can teach you. You have to find it and experience it yourself. I guess that's part of the allure of it. To live. It's part of growing up. Love and a relationship."

Ellie stared at him blankly and started to ask why he was acting weird when Marcus returned. He plopped the water bottles down next to their owners, then sat down next to Ellie.

"What'd I miss?" he asked jokingly.

Ellie smiled at him and shook her head. Her father stared into the hypnotic flames of the campfire. The light flickered across his face like ghosts.

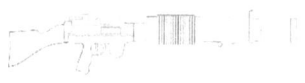

His heart ached. It was not from the strain of hiking but from time marching on. He knew eventually, the day would come, but he was still not prepared for it.

He glanced over at Ellie, wrapped up in her sleeping bag, sewn up and tattered.

He gave her everything he could. And would give even more in a heartbeat if she asked.

His eyes drifted to the campfire again. The rabbit's remains snapped in the embers as it burned away the last remains of sinew and flesh.

He sat in relative silence, remembering all the things that made her happy. How they changed over the years, how she grew up and traded things like blankets for stuffed animals or pillows. The smile they would bring to her face always raised his spirits.

His heart would break when she was sad or when he realized she was growing up so fast. The world was a nasty place, harsh and demanding. It didn't slow down for anyone, especially the girl he would always see as a child playing in the yard, bubbly with giggles.

Ellie suddenly rubbed her nose as if something tickled it, then smacked her lips together and rolled over. He chuckled at the sight.

The fire died out a few hours later, and he woke Ellie up. "It's your turn to watch," he said.

She mumbled incoherently, and he smiled.

"Come on, I need my beauty sleep," he said.

"Won't help," she replied, stretching. Ellie rolled to her side and then sat up, pulling the blankets up around her shoulders. "Fine, get to snoring."

"Thank you, I will," he said as he crawled into his bag and fell quickly asleep.

The next day went by quietly. Each step they took, put them more on edge, as if death awaited them on the other side of each rolling hill. They soon came to another broken highway that ran east and west. They followed it west toward another city's ruins, long abandoned.

"We'll camp here for the night. Get some sleep," Ellie's father said, looking around inside an abandoned building.

Marcus began to follow Ellie but was stopped by Ellie's father with an outstretched hand. "We're in no man's land. I need to know that if shit goes sideways, you'll protect her with your life."

Marcus peered at him, wide-eyed. "Y-yes, of course."

"And yet, you have no weapons?" He sighed, pulled a hunting knife from his belt, and handed it to Marcus. "You make sure you do."

His eyes grew gentle, though his face remained frozen in hard, stern lines.

The night went by quietly. They didn't make a campfire for fear of giving away their position. They sat and ate trail mix and did little talking.

Ellie's father didn't even unroll his bag. Instead, he closed his eyes and tried to sleep sitting up. He drifted off restlessly. The hard ground was uncomfortable, and the smell of death was too close for his comfort. Yet eventually, he did sleep.

He awoke with a start, drew his pistol instinctively, and looked frantically around. Ellie had not woken him. That was his first thought. Then he noticed they were gone.

He scrambled to his feet, kicking dust up as he did, and began to search the area. The pre-dawn light teased his eyes. It gave him enough light to see but not enough to track the footprints in the dirt.

35

His mind raced with possibilities, "Maybe they snuck off. They are teenagers, after all," he told himself. "Yes, that's it. Why would marauders take them and not me? They wouldn't."

He didn't want to yell for them; much like the fire, it would give them all away.

Fear and panic clawed at his guts. He checked the shelter and saw the kids' gear had gone untouched. This led him further to believe they had wandered off willingly. He grabbed the bags, his sword, and Ellie's bow. By then, the sun had spread its warm fingers out over the landscape enough, allowing him to spot the kids' footprints. They had wandered off to the west, toward tall grass nestled against the growing mountain range.

"How long have I slept?" he wondered as he made his way through the grass. He could clearly see their prints. The pair of tracks stopped at a small pond. "Raiders. Oh gods, please, no."

Large boots had stomped through the grass behind the teens' smaller ones. He could not find their shoe prints leading away from the pond. The marauders must have picked them up and carried them back over the hill. He was grateful those prints were easy to find and follow.

He climbed up the mountain where the highway went up a hill and then turned away. The dust was kicked up in places, making it easy to follow the pack of hunters.

The trail dove down into a small valley and then climbed out along a road, past broken-down buildings and vehicles. They were headed north toward the vast emptiness on the other side.

As he made it to the top of the hill, he saw a large village with burning pyres scattered around the outskirts of shacks. Men dressed in broken metal and pieces of leather patrolled nearby.

Ellie's dad backed up slowly and found a ruin nearby that allowed him to watch from the shadows. He buried the bags in some debris in the corner and planned his next move carefully.

He took Ellie's bow and flung the quiver over his head. He slid his sword, sheath and all, into the quiver and checked his pistol. Two clips and 23 rounds left. He wished he hadn't traded so much of his ammo.

It was the dawn of the third day. There was no skulking about the shadows. There was no time to wait for nightfall. He had to find the kids.

Enough boulders, fallen structures, and old vehicles were strewn about that his advance toward the village went unnoticed. As he drew closer, he saw a half dozen marauders poking and laughing at the two teens currently tied up in the middle of town.

A marauder, preoccupied with the smoke rings he tried to blow from his cigarette, drew too close to his position. He pulled the filthy body down and slit the man's throat. The ravager gurgled and then drowned in his own blood.

He rummaged through the marauder's possessions. A sharp piece of metal and other unimaginable pieces of junk that meant nothing to him. Finally, he pulled out a small square box with a lid on one end. He opened it to reveal a wick and a wheel. When he spun the wheel, the wick lit with a click. Ellie's dad smiled.

With a way of creating fire, he walked around, lighting various things ablaze as far away from the two kids as possible. Then he quickly ran back to the north end and waited. He didn't need to wait long. Within a few minutes, the eastern edge of town was burning, and people were running around screaming.

Ducking behind a building, he crept up toward the two kids. There were two guards. *Simple enough to deal with,* he thought. He notched an arrow, with another one in his hand ready to go. With practiced ease, he let loose an arrow, and before the body fell, he had notched and loosed the second. It found its mark and dropped the body soundlessly to the earth. He darted to the kids and quickly cut the bonds around their feet and wrists.

"Shhh," he said, holding a finger up to his lips.

He handed Ellie her bow and quiver but took the sword from it. He motioned for the kids to follow him.

As he shifted around to lead them away, someone screamed an alarm nearby, "Thief! Intruder!"

"Run!" Ellie's father said, pushing the kids north. There was no time now to get the bags.

They ran past the first row of shacks. As they did, the three of them ran into a returning patrol, who started yelling for them to stop.

Ellie's dad growled; he felt it in his lungs. Anger raged in his eyes. He rushed headlong into the band of seven men. He heard his daughter's voice somewhere in the distance, but he couldn't tell what she said. One of the men beside him fell, an arrow protruding from his chest. The sword he had slid from its sheath swung in a blur of silver steel. Two more men died.

There was a bang, which caused him to stumble instinctively, but he kept going. He pulled his pistol and fired a round into the belly of a marauder. His sword sunk into the neck of another.

The village beyond had sent a few more warriors toward them. He glanced over and saw Ellie fire near point-blank into one while Marcus wrestled with another.

They were running out of time. They had to escape. Yanking the sword from the marauder's neck, he turned and shot the two last men down before they could close the distance. He saw two more from the village closing in and dropped them both with a pair of shots.

Ellie shoved an arrow into the neck of the marauder who fought with Marcus. The tip punctured the carotid artery and sprayed blood all over her. Marcus pushed away from the body and scrambled north.

"Run!" Ellie's dad bellowed.

Before they could get far, two more men rushed them. Ellie tried to fend off the first marauder, but it was too late. The other barreled into Ellie's dad as he felt his ribs give with a sickening crack. He fell to the ground, his pistol sliding from his hand and landing in the dirt.

He wrestled with the marauder, hands and legs entwined, each trying to gain the upper hand. There was a bang nearby, then warm blood trickled onto his face--thick, gooey, and metallic.

Ellie's dad pushed the dead marauder to the earth and stood. An arrow stuck out of the man's neck at a low angle. Ellie had shot down through the outlaw's back and into his lungs. He glanced up and saw Marcus holding his pistol. The marauder that had been attacking Ellie lay dead at his feet.

"Go. Run," he said.

The three of them scooped up fallen weapons as they scurried away. They used every ounce of energy they had to escape toward an uncertain future. After a few hours of jogging, they finally slowed and began walking at a rushed pace, ever north. The screams and shouts of protest had faded from their ears as they entered the rolling and rocky landscape surrounding the Lake south of Old Vegas.

"S-stop," Ellie said.

"We can't, not yet. We need to get to the dam," her dad said, breathing heavily. Pain accompanied every breath he took; it stabbed him each time he breathed.

They walked silently for a few more hours before the hills turned steep, and the road, once the lifeline between the states, lay shattered and abandoned. Moving over the rough terrain was becoming more difficult for Ellie's dad. Each crawl over the landscape, each descent, pained him. He could feel his face grow paler with each passing moment.

He stumbled slightly but caught himself with the now-sheathed sword. It acted as a hiking staff as he climbed and a cane when he walked. It gave him balance when his legs grew weak.

They came around a bend in the road and saw below them the remains of a concrete dam, massive and full to the brim. As they walked up to the water, Ellie's dad stopped. His legs could take him no further.

Ellie peered back at him, and he smiled. She had grown up to be the best woman he could have hoped for.

"Dad?" she said, stumbling over to him. "You okay?"

"On the other side is Old Vegas," he gasped.

She looked at him. "I know. We'll be there in a minute. Drink some water?"

"You're beautiful, you know that?" he asked her with a smile. He couldn't hide the grimace that shot across his face, causing her eyes to widen in fear.

Marcus walked over to him and held up his pistol. "Here's your gun, sir."

Ellie's dad closed his tired eyes and shook his head. "It's yours now. Use it to protect one another."

"Look, the guards at the dam are right there, just a bit further. Come on! We're almost there," Ellie said. She walked over to him and took his hand in hers. It was covered in blood--his blood, warm and sticky.

"We all die sometime, Ellie," her dad said.

Her face paled as shock and fear covered her features like a white sheet. "Dad?" Ellie said, squeezing his hand harder.

"I've done all I can for you, Ellie. I've given you everything." He tried to swallow, but his throat was dry. "You have your entire future ahead of you. Over those hills, you'll find what you need to lead a resistance against the Horde. Your future is there, in Old Vegas. You'll be safe with the last of humanity."

"I-I don't want to go alone," she said. "Are you mad at me? Yell at me for wandering off with Marcus... Just...Something!"

Her dad took her face in his bloodied hands and kissed her nose. "Would getting mad at you change anything? There is nothing to be mad at. I don't blame you; you are like me for good or bad. You follow your own path."

"I-I'm sorry," she said. "Please. We can find a doctor in Old Vegas. Just... hang on."

"You have nothing to be sorry for. Old Vegas is your new home. It's the last hope for humanity since Phoenix fell. It was never meant to be mine." Ellie's dad stumbled to a boulder and sat beside it.

She looked at him. He could tell she wanted to argue more. Before she could, he picked up the sword that had dropped to the ground and held it out to her. "You've seen that the Horde can be defeated. You must rally the last bastion of hope for mankind around your banner. Rally them to stand and fight."

She took it, staring at it in disbelief. "I...Help us!" She screamed toward the guards before turning back to him, tears stinging her eyes. He could see anger growing in their brown depths.

The guards ran over to them, one dropping beside Ellie's dad as they approached, as he began to assess his wounds. They began tearing his shirt open, where blood seeped from a gunshot and several lacerations.

"Dad!" Ellie called as Marcus pulled her away to let the soldiers work.

She peered up at her as tears ran down his bloodied face. A proud smile spread across his tired face. "I love you."

They watched as more guards appeared, guiding the young adults away to safety. Because that's what they were now, the two young adults. They would help her dad as best they could, but it would be in vain. Ellie and Marcus were escorted across the span of the dam. He smiled. He had given her everything she needed to survive. To live. To grow. Blood pooled under him, and he sighed. His last thought was of his beautiful daughter, smiling and giggling happily in the warm summer air as she played. He smiled again, with no pain this time, and let out one final breath. The soldiers bowed their heads in reverence.

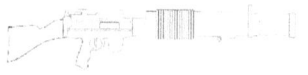

THREE OF SPADES

al shivered involuntarily, causing his shoulder to jerk back. Kira raised her face and cocked her head sideways.

"Sorry, girl," Cal whispered, scratching her head. She sat her head back down on her paws as she waited. Her sharp amber eyes remained fixed on him.

"Tango in the open. Five hundred seventy-six yards. Wind two knots, cross from left." Grant whispered as he adjusted his spotting scope into focus.

Cal looked down his rifle scope at the area they had been watching for the last few days and caught sight of their target. The sun was setting behind them as they hunkered down in the open grasslands at the base of Book Cliffs. The rocky landscape provided cover as long as they remained low and motionless.

"Target confirmed," Cal replied, "Call it."

"Half mil up."

"Half mil up," Cal confirmed.

"One mil left."

Cal clicked the knob on his scope in the correct direction and repeated the command back to Grant.

"Send it," Grant said.

Cal held his breath, then let it out ever so slowly. His vision narrowed to the single point at the other end of his scope, the crosshairs blurring into the target. His finger, ever so lightly touching the trigger on his rifle. It gave way with a smooth crack. The bullet inside exploded with life, and a small puff of hot air escaped the end of the muzzle.

"Good kill," Grant said, clapping Cal on the back in congratulations before standing. "That's now a two of spades."

Cal laughed as he stood and picked up his rifle. He collapsed the bipod before slinging the weapon over a shoulder. Kira sat up and barked once as if she were joining in the revelry.

"Shall we collect your trophy?" Grant said as he started down range toward the target.

The two men, followed closely by Kira, walked toward the Horde-sized metal cutout with a three of spades taped at its center. The middle spade was missing, replaced with a hole where the round had hit it.

Grant laughed and pulled the card off, handing it to Cal. "If what they say in Old Vegas is true, the Horde won't even see us coming."

"It's been years since they moved. Are you really buying what that kid told the council?"

Grant shrugged. "The council believes her. We wouldn't be here otherwise."

Cal nodded and slid the card into his pocket before looking down at Kira, sitting beside him, waiting expectantly. His lifelong companion and fierce guard dog. Her amber eyes sparkled at him. Black and brown two-tone fur covered an athletic and sleek body. She was a mutt, as far as Cal had ever known. No one kept track of the breed of dogs, as they did before the Horde invaded.

"Well, let's get back to camp," Grant said as he looked up at the setting sun.

"We'll set out bright and early tomorrow."

Cal sighed and turned toward the camp with Kira close on his heels. The hike would be long but easy with his two closest friends. He smiled inwardly.

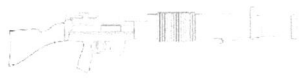

Kira lifted her head, which had been lying on Cal's stomach, and growled slightly before sitting up. She flicked her pink tongue out to lick her muzzle.

"Wake up," Grant said as he poked Cal in the ribs with a worn leather boot.

Cal stirred, stretching his limbs until they became taught. Then grunted and stood. He reached down and gave Kira a scratch behind the ear, which elicited a furious wag. He looked toward the horizon to see the sun hadn't yet broken over the mountains.

Grant followed his gaze before hefting the other strap to his backpack over his shoulder. The two men were equal in height. The only thing that separated them was the muscle that bulged below dark green and brown camouflage fatigues. Cal was tall and agile with blue-green eyes and short black hair, while Grant was stockier, with brown eyes and brown hair.

"We better get moving. Colorado is still a few days' travel. Winter will be moving in soon, and the Horde will be moving with it," Grant said as he picked his rifle up from where it was leaning against his cot.

Cal nodded in agreement and put on his jacket that he had been using as a pillow before throwing his own pack on. He picked up his rifle and slid the bolt back slightly to check that a round had been chambered before slamming it closed again. "All set."

Grant made his way out of the tent to the mess hall a few yards away. The two men sat down and were served hot coffee and as much bacon, bread, and eggs as they could fit in their mouths. Kira stood next to Cal, where she awaited slivers of the salty pork. She looked disappointed when Cal kicked the bowl of food next to her with the toe of a boot. Cal knew she should be eating her own meal but couldn't help sharing a few of the salty morsels after several pleading looks of starvation from his furry companion.

The camp they were stationed at was sparsely manned, and they were the only ones currently eating. Their location was a forward ranger station at the edge of the desert. The only safe area this far north and east. It was a few miles west of the Horde's territory. They were sent here to find out the current location of the Horde and report back on any recent westward movement. For years the Horde had stayed away from the dry, hot deserts of the southwest until recently.

"You ready?" Grant asked in-between chewing the rest of his bread and standing.

Cal stuffed the last slice of bacon in his mouth and rose, wiping the grease on his pants before standing. He nodded in response.

They gathered their gear and began the long, tiring hike east. The stony giants of the Colorado Rockies loomed in the distance as the sun sparked up over the horizon, causing the rocky crags to become backlit silhouettes.

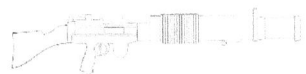

The temperature had dropped noticeably the higher they got and the deeper into Colorado they traveled. What was left of the highway, once known as the I-70, was broken and overgrown. Nature had long since reclaimed the land and the resources that made up the shattered road.

"You ever read those books about the old days, the ones in the archives? The ones that were written by important people?" Cal asked as they hiked along the grey top of the highway.

Grant thought a moment, then shrugged his broad shoulders. "Not really. I was more into the superhero stuff."

Cal laughed.

"What? Don't tell me you never read those growing up," Grant snickered.

"Oh, I did," Cal replied. "But I also grew up."

Grant snorted. "Right, and I grew an extra set of arms. Who reads history books? Nerd."

Cal looked at him and smiled. "You are pretty ugly. I'm sure you mutated somehow."

Grant narrowed his eyes at him in mock outrage. "You read the apocalypse comics, didn't you."

Their laughter echoed off the buttes that flanked them, lifting the weight of the dying world around them, if only for a moment.

"I sure do miss being a kid, though," Cal said with a smile as the horror of reality settled over their mirth.

"It was a simpler time, wasn't it? Living in Old Vegas, getting in trouble with that local store owner. God, what was his name?"

"Frank."

"Yeh, that was it. Man, he did not like us rummaging around his shelves looking for candy."

"Nope," Cal replied with a chuckle. He shifted his rifle to the other shoulder. His eyes never left Kira, who was several yards ahead of them. "Or, what about Jeanene."

"Oh, man. Yeh, Jeanene Forrith," Grant said with a wistful sigh.

Cal sighed mournfully and nodded. "Such a hottie. We had such a crush on her."

"Yeah."

The two men were silent for a moment as the ghosts of their past fluttered through their mind's eyes. Like frames of a motion comic, the images flipped through their mind as if someone thumbed through the pages of their life.

"I remember when she died and feeling like the world truly didn't want such a wonderful thing to be subjected to the kind of hell life we've had to live."

"Yeah," Cal replied.

The sun had set behind them, and the last rays of orange gripped the edge of the horizon as if protesting its eventual descent into darkness. The cold evening air bit hard against the men's exposed skin. A long stretch of road climbed up before them, marking the edge of the valley they were in and the higher mountain and forests of the Rockies. The smell of damp earth and pine was foreign to their desert-born noses. It felt refreshing but also sent goose pimples across their skin. As if something primal resonated in their bones with their surroundings, urging them to hunt.

"We'd better camp here for the night," Grant said, looking at the steep curving highway.

Kira stopped, sniffed the road ahead, then returned to Cal's side.

"She seems to agree with you."

"That's never a good sign."

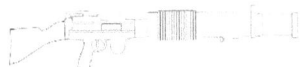

The campfire died hours before dawn. The men slept very little and took turns guarding their small camp during the night. It would be the last time they would have a fire of any kind for a while, and instead would huddle together for warmth. Heavy clouds skimmed the peaks, smothering everything with a canopy of grey and gloomy blankets. They threatened to drench them in ice, cold rain, and snow. The two men ate quickly and quietly before heading up the steep cliffs.

Kira took the lead once again, her ears listening intently to the still and quiet forest. She stopped every so often to smell the road, causing the two men to freeze, and take a knee. Their rifles were poised against their shoulder in reflex, ready for anything.

When the area was clear, they continued further into the darkened forests of the Colorado Rockies.

Dusk settled over them, and they spent their first night huddled under a pine tree, eating cold pieces of food from a can. Kira rested her head on Cal's thigh and watched. The next morning, they forged on through the wilderness. No one spoke, and they whispered only when absolutely necessary, instead relying mostly on hand gestures.

Trees towered above them like a wall of wooden Phalanx. Browns and greens were muted, echoing the dread that crept into their hearts with each step. They were getting closer. Broken down tanks, trucks, and other military vehicles lay abandoned and broken along the road. Stripped and forgotten after so many years. The signs of the Horde began to appear as their alien tech, once shiny and new, was also broken and forgotten in heaps across the mountainside.

Grant held his rifle tighter, turning his knuckles white on the rifle's grip, ready to spring into action.

Cal fidgeted, running his thumb up and down the length of the rifle grip. While the wilderness around them hadn't changed, the air somehow had. It had become laced with an almost acidic undertone, just enough to be detectible.

Kira had stopped a split second before Grant called for them to halt their march. He heard noises in the distance. He moved a hand to the dense forest, and both Cal and Kira followed close behind.

As they lay motionless in the damp earth, the smell of decayed leaves and wet earth wafted into their noses. The sound of the Horde grunting and speaking in their broken tongues floated down the highway toward them. Kira lay between them, her ears listening intently.

They wore a patchwork of broken armor, leftovers from the original siege on the east and western coasts. Their massive hands carried rifles that were not made on Earth. Large bored barrels with electrified fields of blue rippled mesmerizingly.

Cal set a calming hand on Kira. The creature's cackles caused the fur on her neck to stand on end in spiked clusters down her back.

The patrol of Horde passed by, unaware of their presence. The two men waited for several minutes before rising to one knee. They cleared their surroundings before carefully melting back away from the highway, disappearing further into the thick underbrush and bracken of the forest.

Stepping through the wilderness was slower. Each foot was placed purposefully to avoid sound as much as possible.

The two men and the canine carefully picked their way through the mountainside shrubs in search of an overlooking perch to view the town a few miles away. They could make out the Horde in the valley even through the trees. Their bulk was stark against the ruins of the city's black and grey backdrop.

"We need to get closer; we can't make out details from here," Cal whispered from his kneeling position, his eyes focused down the scope.

Grant nodded, then motioned for Cal to follow. Kira zig-zagged her way ahead of them, darting from tree to tree.

They got as close as they dared and set up a blind between two trees and boulders. They dug in quietly, then piled pine branches on top to hide their presence. It allowed them just enough space to lie down. Cal was able to position his rifle in front of them while Grant set up a spotting scope next to him. Their proximity kept them warm while Kira paced nervously outside.

The two men set about their respective tasks. Cal took notes while Grant set about calculating distances and a kill zone. After several hours, the sun began to set, plunging them into darkness. Kira crawled between the two men, boosting the warmth they shared.

Cal adjusted his body on the rolled-out sleeping mat. His sleeping bag was draped over his shoulders. He opened a pack of food and began to eat. He poured some water from his canteen into a small cup and sat it down in front of Kira, who lapped it up greedily. Cal reached into his pocket and took out the three of spades, running a thumb over the hole in the center, where the middle spade had been before being shot out. He smiled and put it back before taking another bite of food. Grant was focused on his spotting scope pointed at the city.

Cal scratched Kira's ear as she licked her lips. She had been his companion for so long. He draped an arm around her neck and lay his head down on his folded arm. Kira had come into his life right before he joined the Militia Scouts. There wasn't much argument about allowing Kira to go through training with him. She guarded him fiercely, even as a puppy. It had been cute until she was older and much bigger. Then it became a trait he enjoyed. Only Grant, his lifelong friend, was ever allowed to get close to Cal.

Cal smiled at the memory and gripped a handful of her fur. She smelled of earth and a unique dog smell. It was comforting and familiar in the cold darkness of the forest. His shoulders eased, and he passed into an uneasy slumber, leaving Grant and Kira awake for guard duty.

Grant woke him a few minutes before dawn. The first thing he noticed was the rush of cold air as Kira crawled from their hiding spot, leaving his side exposed to the air. A shiver ran down his back as he began to stretch at least as much as he could in his prone position. Daylight would be his watch, and it was the most dangerous. Where Grant had to worry about anyone getting close enough to hear them, Cal had to worry about that, plus the added sense of sight. Although their hiding spot was well hidden, a trained eye could still spot them if they were looking. He hoped no one was.

The rustling of a food package caused him to glare at Grant, who only offered a small shrug as if to say "sorry."

Cal shook his head and returned to his observations. The Horde in the distance were quiet and unconcerned, with the sniper team within shooting distance. Soldiers stacked crates near one of their caravan trucks, a large, green, and grey machine that looked as ugly as its owners. Enslaved men under the service of the Horde went about their chores, occasionally prodded by a taskmaster's sharp tongue. Although he couldn't hear them, Cal knew the language was guttural and foreign.

A low growl broke him from the monotony of watching the city. Goosebumps prickled his skin, and he looked back over his shoulder to the small opening of the hide. Kira was standing at the entrance with her back to them.

"Kira," Cal whispered softly. She stopped and crawled into the hide. Cal reached over and shook Grant, who stirred awake, grabbing his rifle instinctively.

Grant shot him a glance. Cal only pointed toward the exit, then pulled his sidearm from its holster. He knew there was a round already in the chamber. They were too deep in enemy territory for rookie mistakes. Grant shouldered his carbine rifle and pointed it toward the exit. They could now hear heavy footsteps drawing closer.

Cal slowed his breathing as much as he could without raising his heartbeat. The footsteps paused a moment. *Had they spotted the hide?* Cal wondered as his finger set firmly against the pistol's trigger.

Seconds seemed like hours before the footsteps continued and then moved away into the distance.

After several more moments, Cal relaxed slightly and lowered his gun, which Grant did as well. The two men looked at one another. Relief was clearly visible on their dirt-stained faces. Kira shook herself, causing dust to cloud the hide. Both men's eyes widened as the dust began to tickle their noses. They scratched it in hopes of tricking it into not sneezing, which luckily worked. Cal looked at his Canine companion reprovingly.

Grant turned back around to the lookout and set his rifle down while Kira crawled from the exit hole. Cal sighed and holstered his pistol before turning back around to look down the scope toward the city. *That was too close,* he thought to himself.

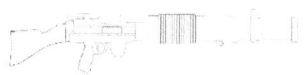

The sun was setting, casting long shadows across the forest. Lights hadn't started to come on. The town's lack of obstructed views meant that the sun's rays could freely illuminate the ruins, granting Cal a clear shot across the area.

His scope settled on a new area of the Horde's camp which had become busy in the last few hours. Horde soldiers began to pile into the city in general, but this makeshift command center was nothing more than a burnt-out hotel lobby. Reinforcements from the west began to trickle in, causing a buzz of activity.

Cal reached over and woke Grant again, who started for his rifle. Cal shook his head and pointed toward the spotting scope.

Grant crawled into position and scanned the city, settling on the area Cal had observed.

The two men began to write fervently in their small notepads, counting troops as well as the type of supplies and other logistical information. But the sudden appearance of a Horde Mech caused the men to inhale sharply.

It was a hulk of a military machine, reaching the height of some of the three-story buildings, with a sleek metallic body and assortment of external weapons, including missiles and laser banks.

Grant looked at Cal and whispered, "They're staging for an invasion."

Cal nodded in agreement.

"High-value target, near the mech's leg. Yards, one four niner four," Grant said softly, as he adjusted his scope before writing some numbers down on a piece of paper in front of him.

Cal moved the scope in the desired direction and spotted a burly pilot standing next to an even larger creature. "Commander and a mech pilot," he said under his breath before shooting Grant a look. Their orders were to observe and report back. However, they were also given secondary instructions that any high-priority targets be dealt with swiftly. Mech pilots were increasingly rare after years of war.

"We have to take the shot before it's too late," Grant whispered. "Wind at target, right, 3 knots."

Cal took a deep breath and let it out slowly. He moved his scope crosshairs from the field commanders' head to the pilots and back again. He counted seconds between the movement, then repeated it again as if committing the movement to muscle memory. Consecutive shots were extremely difficult on a good day. Let alone in the middle of enemy territory. One misjudgment could mean their exposure and, worse still, missing one or both targets.

"Left three clicks. Up, two," Grant whispered.

Cal made the necessary adjustment on his scope, then set his finger lightly on the trigger. His vision narrowed to a single point at the center of the crosshairs. His breathing slowed.

"Send it," he heard Grant say.

Cal pulled the trigger and sent two rounds down range to their target. The mech pilot and field commander fell to the ground with a jerk of their heads within a second of one another.

Chaos erupted in the camp. A rush of Horde soldiers charged into the forest. The men would no longer be safe in their hiding spot.

The two men packed their notepads and the spotting scope and crawled from the hide. Cal did the same, pulling his rifle along with him. He threw his jacket and backpack on before chambering another round in his rifle. "Where's Kira?"

"I don't know, I'm sure she's fine, come on," Grant said before jumping down from their overlook and heading deeper into the woods.

Cal followed reluctantly. He didn't dare call or whistle for her. Doing so would give their position away. The two men made their way down the mountain as quickly and quietly as possible. They stuck to the lengthening shadows of the tall pine trees, heading back toward the highway.

"Wait," Cal said abruptly as he dropped to one knee. Grant stopped and scanned the tree line. "We can't go back the way we came. The road will be watched. We'll never make it that way."

"Shit, you're right."

Cal pulled out a map from his pocket and unfolded it. He gave it a quick scan and then pointed west. "We have to stick to the hills as much as possible. It's our best option for cover."

Grant looked off in the distance and saw the lower, rolling hills below them. "We'll be sitting ducks out there."

"It's our only chance. We'll stay up here as much as we can until the cover of darkness. Maybe we can lose them there if we can get to the river."

Grant clenched his jaw, then nodded.

Cal pocketed the map before they climbed their way along the mountainside, only descending as much as they thought safe or where they were forced to. The hillside became steeper the further west they went. If they dropped too far, they would leave the relative safety of the trees for the smaller conifer shrubs that dotted the foothills and valley below.

It would be dark soon, and they would need to either camp or risk the hike with no light. They could hear shouts in the distance.

Grant stopped this time and looked down a steep decline along the mountain. "We have to descend from here. We'll be in the open," he said.

Cal nodded in response. "It's not going to matter soon. We'll be better off down there if we can keep out of sight until nightfall."

Grant nodded once, then climbed down. Rocks scattered and rolled down the mountain. Cal watched as Grant carefully climbed down, then shouldered his rifle and looked back toward the tree line. *Where is Kira?* he thought before climbing down behind Grant.

The two men turned down the hill and sprinted the remaining distance to the large, rolling hills of the valley. Sporadic shrubs, boulders, and trees covered the green lowlands of the mountains while the sun ahead of them began to sink below the horizon. The men rounded a rocky outcropping and came to an abrupt halt. Two large Horde creatures growled and raised their rifles at them.

Grant, already in a position to fire, got off two shots, killing one of them before they could react. The second grotesque green creature fired into Grant's chest, sending his companion reeling back. Before Cal could raise his own weapon, Kira darted from a nearby bush and launched herself at the creature's arm. The Horde howled in rage and pain as Kira's teeth sunk in. Before it could retaliate, Cal pulled his pistol and shot twice into the creature's face. The back of the Horde's head exploded, painting the rocks behind it with blood and gore.

Cal kneeled beside Grant, who was staring blankly at the sky above. "Damn, you. Damn it!"

Anger and loss trickled down his cheeks in salty rivulets. Kira came over and sniffed Grant before licking his dirty face once, then twice. She looked up at Cal as if expecting an answer to a question she didn't know how to ask. "He's gone," Cal said through clenched teeth.

Shouts further north and east broke him of his reverence. He dropped his rifle, picked up Grant's, and then pulled the spare magazines from Grant's pack and stashed them away in his pockets. He then stood and looked down at his friend's lifeless body one more time. "I'm sorry," Cal said, bowing his head.

The rock above him exploded from a rifle round, causing Cal to duck and then jump for cover near the outcropping. The Horde was closing in fast. He fired several shots in the direction of the advancing Horde. Grant's rifle was perfect for close combat, but they were still too far for consistent accuracy. His heart thundered loudly in his ears, nearly drowning out the explosions from the rifle as he fired two more rounds toward the Horde. Kira lay beside his leg as if hiding from the loud noises.

Cal could see two of the Horde trying to flank him. He shot them, dropping them to the ground, then he turned his attention back to the advancing creatures. He couldn't stay here. Cal looked over his shoulder and saw another cliff several yards away. He picked his bag up, shouldered it on, then shot twice before bolting from his hiding spot like a rabbit. Kira was close on his heels.

The sound of bullets flying overhead whistled by, like hornets of death flying through the air. Cal stumbled and rolled to the edge of the cliff, then crawled the remaining distance before pulling himself over the edge. He immediately regretted the tactic. Cal slid headfirst into the rocks and low brush of the steep decline. He tried to tuck himself up and only managed to roll sideways before bouncing off a boulder. Stars flashed across his vision as pain shot through his chest and ribs.

When he stopped rolling and sliding, dust clogged his lungs and coated his mouth. Blood had mixed into the dirt, turning it into metallic-tasting mud. He spat it out and tried to take a deep breath but couldn't. His lungs were on fire. Tears washed streaks on his face as his body tried to cleanse the dust from his eyes. He lay motionless, his heart hammering loudly in his ears, causing the pain in his lungs to pulse with each heartbeat.

Move, he told himself. *You have to move.*

Kira stood next to him, her ears listening intently, though he could tell she wasn't paying him any attention. She was focused on the cliff above him.

Cal grunted as he pushed himself up, pain and nausea washing over him like an engulfing tidal wave. He tried to force it down and managed to get to one knee before spitting bile. Kira growled beside him. The fur on the nape of her neck stood up in warning.

They were closer than he thought. Or had he passed out? He wasn't sure. He stood shakily, then stumbled forward toward a nearby bush. He peered through the conifers toward the cliff above. He didn't see the Horde, but it didn't mean they weren't there. They would spot him if they looked down. He had to put as much distance between himself and them as he could.

Cal looked west toward the setting sun and saw mostly open grasslands. There was little hope of hiding in the open, and he couldn't stay hidden for long in the brush. He looked down at Kira, who was still fixated on the cliff, though she had stopped growling. "Come on, girl, I guess we have no choice. We have to move."

He leveled the rifle at the edge of the cliff in anticipation and backed away slowly westward, checking over his shoulder as he went to ensure he didn't stumble over a rock or uneven ground. With each footstep, he grew more and more confident they hadn't seen him fall over the edge. After several minutes of this, he finally turned and jogged away west toward the setting sun.

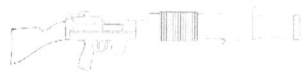

The pain kept him awake, but the cold spurred him on. He had lost track of time. Only a singular, primal need to survive coaxed one more step forward, then another. Dusk had left heavy clouds in the sky, and he prayed, to whatever god that was listening, that it didn't rain.

Kira stopped ever so often and looked behind them as if she could sense their imminent danger. Although Cal saw nothing, he knew her senses were far better.

Cal could not move one more step, and he stumbled forward, barely catching himself on one knee before hitting the ground. He moaned in pain.

He pulled his pack off and set it down, rummaging around for his canteen. He drank deeply. He rinsed his mouth and spat rehydrated blood and dirt onto the ground. He poured some water for Kira, who lapped at it eagerly.

He pulled the magazine from the rifle, checking his ammo supply. "Five rounds left and two mags in reserve," he said. Kira responded with a tilt of her head. "I wouldn't last long in a sustained fight." He put the ammo away and pulled out the map from his pocket. The three of spades he had kept there fell to the ground. He looked at it and pursed his lips. He picked it up and studied it for a moment, then took a pen out and wrote on it. He looked at Kira and then at the card. He folded the card and stuck it in the pouch Kira had on her collar. It was small and could only hold a note or two. But it was watertight, something he had made for getting messages back to camp when they were training for scouting missions back home. He sighed with despair. He never thought he'd have use for this.

Cal turned his attention back to the map. He was days away from the Utah border, and a river stood between him and the interstate that ran west and south. If he could make it to the river tonight, he might stand a chance at staying alive. Cal folded the map and slid it back into his pocket, then looked at Kira with heavy eyes. "We'd better go."

She licked her lips from the water she had drank and watched him as he stood with a painful grimace etched across his features.

He pushed himself forward, setting each foot down carefully in front of the other before continuing through the darkness. Sweat stung his eyes despite the cold air hitting him. Minutes turned to hours as he stumbled through the darkness. Kira stopped every so often and looked back toward Cal, waiting for him to catch up. The pain in his chest caused his vision to narrow every time he took an unexpected step or lost his footing.

Cal stopped once again as the sun began to stretch up over the eastern sky, sending orange strands of light out over the valley. He took another drink from his canteen. He could smell the damp earth mixed with the fresh pine smell that blew down through the mountains. The sound of rushing water grew louder as they drew closer to it.

Shouts interrupted his thoughts, causing him to drop the drinking canister and raise his weapon in the direction of the shouts. The Horde had spotted him in the pre-dawn light. He became careless.

They were close. Cal fired several rounds, hitting two of the creatures in the neck and chest. The rifle let off a loud metallic ping sound, and with years of reflexes and training, he dropped the magazine with the push of a button before slamming another into position. He fired several more rounds, hitting one in the leg and the other in the arm.

"Stay!" Cal commanded, causing Kira to freeze as she readied herself to bolt toward the Horde. "Return!"

Kira did so quickly, taking up position next to Cal's left leg. He backed away toward the water, firing several more shots at the Horde. They were pinned down, but that wouldn't last. Cal swallowed hard, forcing the pain and terror back down.

"Go, run home!" Cal yelled. Kira jumped into action and darted to the bank of the river, splashing into it with abandon.

Cal backed away, covering her as she swam across. The rifle pinged empty once again, and he swiftly reloaded. But it didn't fire. He hadn't hit it hard enough, and it jammed. "Shit," he looked up in time to see several Horde leap up and fire in his direction. A round hit him in the leg, and he stumbled back, dropping the rifle. He panicked and stumbled forward toward the water. He could see Kira shaking the water from her fur on the other side, her eyes fixed on his. "Run!" he screamed. She looked west as if she were going to go but stopped to look back.

Cal felt the second round hit him. It punched him like a fist slamming into his back and burned. He splashed into the water. He would never make it. Fear blanched his face, and his eyes locked onto Kira's. "Go," he said. "Go home." He pulled his pistol from its holster and turned to face the approaching Horde. He fired several shots at them, but it was no good. Several more of their rounds hit him, sending him reeling backward into the water. Blood flowed down the swiftly moving ice-cold brown and grey water. Cal's mind drifted into nothingness as he floated for several seconds before passing out and slipping below the gentle current of the river.

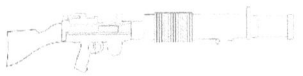

The sun was starting to set, and dinner had been served to the remaining rangers at the outpost. The camp chef, endearingly called Cookie, scrubbed the cast iron skillet lovingly. It had been cold, and rain had been heavy on the eastern horizon. It would start to get even colder, he thought as he wiped the blackened ash from the pot. He poured some oil into it and then wiped it out. "There," he said to no one and then hung the pot up. He took a deep breath and closed his eyes in a job well done, then opened them swiftly. He could smell blood and wet dog.

He looked around but didn't see anything, then looked under the table to find a wet and scratched canine with black and brown swaths of fur. He recognized it as Kira, Cal's companion. "It's ok, girl," Cookie said cautiously, his eyes wide in surprise. He turned and filled a bowl with water and set it down in front of her.

She didn't move. She lay there, looking up at him with tired eyes.

"Hey, commander!" Cookie called.

"Yeh?" Commander Harris walked into the circle of tables and saw the scroungy and malnourished dog lying near a bench. "Is that… Kira?"

Harris knelt beside her and sent a gentle hand down on her head. She made no move to fight him. She didn't even whimper. She lay there, blinking at him with scared and sad amber orbs. "It's ok, girl, we've got you." Harris looked up at the chef, who shrugged, "Get the medic."

Cookie nodded and disappeared around the kitchen tent.

Harris felt for the collar buried in her fur and unzipped the small pouch hidden there. He pulled the folded three of spades from it. He carefully unfolded the card and read the warning: "They're coming!"

LOSSES

Waves of heat emitted from the broken blacktop outside the gate. Sand blew across the shattered surface, pushing along discarded paper and tumbleweeds. A reflection of emptiness that blanketed the Western country. The air was hot and stale, while the sand choked anyone dumb enough to wander the wastes outside the city. Ellie stood at the Old Vegas gates, looking along what was once the busiest street in the state. At least, that's what she had read. It had been decades since the last remnants of human survivors on the west coast settled here, hidden among the giant towers of broken steel, concrete, and glass. A once lively city diminished to rubble and shattered dreams, far beyond its original machinations.

She brushed a lock of brown hair back from her face and turned around to find Marcus standing nearby, a rifle slung over his shoulder.

"We heard from the eastern front?" he asked.

Once full of youth, her weathered face was now scarred with survival lessons. The tip of one ear held a crevice where she had fallen off a cliff. Innocence has since faded from her, and she was now entrenched if the hardship of life. Her shoulders slumped from the weight of a life dedicated to tough decisions. She pulled down the scarf covering her nose and mouth. "No, not yet," she replied.

Marcus walked over to her and put a hand on her shoulder. "Come on, let's go inside. Won't do any good to stand out here in the heat waiting for something that may never come."

She sighed and nodded. They walked toward the entrance to the hotel and casino that they used as a homestead. What might have been a beautiful sight once, was now hollowed out and repurposed to support long-term living. The lower levels had become utilitarian, with food, water, and governance taking up most of the room, along with a dining hall and a trade area. Survivors tended to their chores, oblivious to the downcast eyes of their youngest leaders.

Marcus and Ellie had only recently joined the council of leaders. They were elected after leading a large band of refugees from the northeast to Vegas, reportedly killing several of the Horde.

Ellie stopped and glanced up at the vaulted ceiling of the hotel lobby. She peered at Marcus, who was removing his scarf from around his face; a smile warmed his features.

"It'll be ok," Marcus said.

"Will it?"

He nodded.

Ellie slid her hands around Marcus and squeezed him tightly. She lay her head on his chest and inhaled his smell. The scent of dry desert sand and male musk wafted through her nose. She peered up at his brown eyes and opened her mouth to speak but was interrupted by a commotion near the front doors.

Armed guards poured out of their posts toward the gate. Screams of panic and shouts echoed through the lobby. Ellie left the safety of the embrace for the chaos.

The gate into the streets was open, and several guards were lined up, their rifles pointed into the desert landscape.

A group of scouts were following behind five creatures of the Horde. Their usually glistening, thick skin was dry and grey-green. Their heads were downcast as they shuffled through the gates. The guards began yelling orders and pointing their guns at them, forcing the invaders to the ground.

"William, over here," Ellie called.

The lanky scout nodded and walked over to Marcus and Ellie, slinging his rifle over his shoulder.

"What's going on?" she asked.

"We found them marching west. There had been ten or more. This is all that survived," William said.

"They don't look like warriors," Ellie said.

William shook his head. "No, they surrendered to us as we approached."

"What happened to the other half then?" Marcus asked.

"Most of them died on the way here; the desert has always been a barrier to them," William replied.

Shouts from the guards snapped their attention toward the chaos surrounding the captives. Over the decades, they had only managed to learn a minimal amount of the Hordes language. Mostly commands of obedience. One of the Horde, the largest of the group, was growling and thrusting his hands out. Not understanding what was happening, the men shouted back, their fingers firmly planted on the triggers of their rifles.

Ellie watched the scene unfold as if it were a motion picture from the time before the invasion. The creature, still holding his hands out, yelled and tried to get up by crawling away back toward the gate. The other four Horde began shouting in a swirl of broken English, grunts, and growls. Confused, the guards started hitting them and forcing them to the ground with the butt end of their rifles. This caused the larger one to get up and defend the others. As it did, the guards shot him several times. The creature's body slumped to the ground in a pool of green blood. The other four Horde began sobbing and pulling at the dead creature toward them.

"Get them locked up," William said.

Ellie glanced sidelong at Marcus and then back at the Horde. The guards pulled the creatures to their feet and dragged them off toward the prison inside the hotel.

"What the hell is going on?" Marcus said before turning to Ellie.

"The group we found mostly died as we marched west. I'm actually surprised they made it here," William said, returning his attention to Ellie and Marcus. "But the fact they spoke broken English, that's new."

"But why? Why would they risk the desert sands to come here? Knowing they wouldn't all make it?" Ellie asked. She slid a hand around Marcus's arm.

William shrugged. "I don't know."

"What are we going to do with them?" Marcus asked, looking between Ellie and the scout.

Ellie glanced at him, lost in thought. A cloud passed across her face, darkening her usually optimistic outlook. She shook her head in resignation. She pursed her lips before turning to follow the Horde captives into the hotel.

The prison was located downstairs at the back of a stage where cages were once used to house large animals. Now, they are used mostly to hold violent offenders. Those who would rather do harm to their fellow man than save it. Ellie walked up the steps and disappeared behind the pillars, hanging ropes, and what was left of the curtains that were once vibrant and full of color. Various dolls sat discarded on shelves. Their faces were ghostly hollow, and devoid of emotion, like discarded remnants of what they used to be. Her boots echoed on the wooden floor. The auditorium was still used for addresses and the occasional show. With so few people interested, there were fewer of the latter, however.

Ellie descended below the stage to the concrete and brick holding cells. Four steel cages sat on either side of what was once a loading dock, now sealed off to the street above. The four creatures huddled in the corner of the far cage, whispering in soft clicks and groans. The guards, who were talking idly nearby, nodded to her as she approached.

She pulled a chair from a table over to the cage, sat down, facing the Horde inside, and peered at them with hard, cold eyes. She ignored the stares of the guards behind her.

"Can you understand me?" Ellie asked.

The older-looking creature, more feminine than the others, glanced up at her and nodded.

"How much can you understand?"

The creature stared at her momentarily and then looked away, pulling the smallest one back into a tight embrace.

"I think you understand me alright. What I really want to know is, why are you here?"

"Tired," it said, with a guttural groan, as if it forced itself to answer.

"Tired? Of what? Slaughtering our people?" Ellie spat.

The Horde didn't respond.

Ellie stood quickly, knocking over the chair. "Answer me!"

"Everything ok?" one of the guards asked from behind her.

Ellie turned with a start and glared at him. Her hand on her dad's pistol holstered at her side. She clenched her jaw, feeling the muscles bulge at the strain. The guard took a step back. Ellie growled and stormed out of the holding area, oblivious to the looks of concern from the guards.

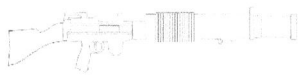

Ellie paced back and forth in her room. She was angry, sure, but why? The Horde were monsters, ones she had spent her adult life exterminating. Why did these prisoners irritate her?

Marcus opened the door and stepped inside, closing it behind him. She turned and glared at him, causing his eyes to widen in surprise.

"What?" she asked.

"Uhm… What, what?" he replied.

"Not in the mood," she said.

"I can see that. Why?" he said, walking over to her. He pulled her close.

Being close to him cooled her fiery temper to a dull smolder. This gnawed at her, and she pushed away. "Did you know I had a grandfather?"

Marcus shook his head.

"I did. He was a pilot during the start of the war. He sacrificed himself to destroy one of the Horde's fighter jets. My dad-"she broke off her sentence. The thought of her dad came back to her in a wash of emotions.

"Ellie?" Marcus asked.

"I-It's been a while since I've thought of my dad," Ellie said, her voice shaking as the last of her anger melted away, leaving her unstable. "I-I miss him."

"Are you ok?" Marcus asked, looking at her with a raised brow.

She took a deep breath and let it out in a controlled hiss. "Yeh, I'm sorry for snapping at you."

"It's ok. Want to talk about it?"

"No, I need to talk to William," she said. She reached for the door, opened it, and disappeared down the hall before Marcus could ask any further questions.

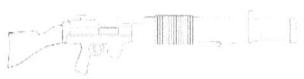

Ellie slid the chair from the table back to sit in front of the cage. She sat heavily, though completely unintentionally. It was as if the world was pressing down on her. She sighed and looked at the Horde in the cage. They still huddled in the corner; wide green eyes stared at her expectedly.

"You came from Colorado, didn't you?" she asked.

The creature nodded. Its face was haggard, with several deep wrinkles and a frozen mask of sorrow.

Ellie pursed her lips and then sat back in the chair. "During my first year as a council member here, I signed the order to send two scout snipers east for the first time in a decade. Their deaths weigh on me each day since. It was the first time I sent men to die. I hated it. I still do. I spoke to William, the scout who found you. He said you guys had come from the city in which we lost those sniper scouts. Or at least close to it."

"Friends?" the creature asked.

Ellie's eyes widened in surprise but then returned to a stoic mask before answering. "No, they weren't. Are you familiar with the meaning?"

"Yes. Like family," the creature said, hugging the smallest creature tighter.

"Is he your kid?" Ellie said, jutting her chin at the creature in her lap.

"Yes."

"Why are you here?"

"Dying."

Ellie arched a brow. "From the desert?"

The creature shook its head. "We not mean to come here."

"Here? You mean Old Vegas?"

"Earth."

Ellie studied the creature for a moment. Its skin was even more pale than it was previously. Although the sub-basement was cool, and water had been given to them, it looked worse off than when it was captured. But it's the revelation of not coming to earth on purpose perplexed her. She didn't know what to think.

"You're dying?"

"Hungry, thirsty, lost," it replied.

"So are we," Ellie said.

The two looked at one another for what seemed like a lifetime. Ellie leaned forward, her hands clasped together, and broke the uneasy silence. "What do you want from us?"

"Freedom."

Ellie snorted in contempt and sat back. "Welcome to the land of freedom." She stood, pulled the chair back to the table, and then turned to face the Horde in the cage. "We used to think you immortal. You came here, whether by accident or not. And slaughtered my people. You lay siege to our entire world. Now you come here, to the city of Sin, and expect what? Mercy?"

The creature stared at her unblinkingly and then turned its attention to the stirring kid on her lap as it woke in a fit of groans.

Ellie shook her head and stomped off toward the stairs.

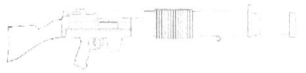

The meeting room was thick with tobacco smoke. The other council members enjoyed smoking during meetings, claiming it calmed their anxious nerves. Ellie found it disgusting and hated the time spent debating meeting topics. She wasn't a politician, relying on instinct and action more than thinking and talking. It was her dad in her, she realized. Twice in as many days, his visage popped into her memory. She missed him.

"He was right," Ellie muttered.

"What's that?" Kelly asked from her place at the table.

"Nothing, just remembering my father," Ellie replied.

"If the Horde know they can reach us now, we're in trouble," Berry said from across the table.

Matt, who was beside him, nodded. "They had attempted to breach the sand barrier before, in Phoenix."

"And succeeded in reaching it," Ellie pointed out. "I was there."

"Yes, but they immediately retreated back to the cooler northeast," Matt replied.

"Then how do we know these are not spies?" Berry asked.

"We don't," Kelly replied.

"We should send our scouts back out, see if their army is waiting for us in Colorado," Matt said.

Marcus, who was on the other side of Ellie, sat forward. "We already know they are, and as of our last reports, they are greatly diminished in number."

"How do we know they aren't hiding?" Berry asked.

Ellie sighed. "They aren't. They are dying."

Everyone at the table turned their attention to her.

"My dad used to say the Horde were not mindless and even had a family. He used to tell me they could be killed, and now we know they are weak. He was right about... A lot of things. Maybe he was right about family?" Ellie said, looking into the eyes of everyone staring at her.

"Even if he was, what does that even mean?" Marcus asked.

"You don't believe me?" Ellie said, feeling her face flush with anger.

"No, I do. I'm trying to understand where that leaves us," Marcus replied, looking at her compassionately.

She mumbled and sat back in her chair. She didn't know what it meant. It used to be easy to hate her dad, sitting in her room, angry with him for making her learn how to hunt, cook, and even debate. Now, she didn't feel hate but frustration. She should have learned more when she had the chance. She had no idea how to handle the Horde in the cells downstairs. Judging by the continued bickering around the table, neither did the rest of them.

William burst through the door, panting. "Guys, the Horde. They are approaching from the northeast."

Marcus and Ellie stood, nearly knocking over their chairs. The others, more politicians than soldiers, glanced around fearfully. Just then, the sound of alarms echoed through the hallowed halls of the hotel.

Ellie stood on the shipping container that acted as a platform along the wall, giving them the ability to look out over the ruined city around them. The Horde could be seen further down the road, milling about with no sense of urgency.

William climbed the ladder and stood beside Ellie and Marcus. "Scouts say there are at least a couple hundred. Armed, but not what they used to be. It's almost like they are guerilla fighters. Certainly not what we've seen before."

"If that's true, we don't know what their capabilities are then. Given our current state, we could maybe hold off a week," Marcus said.

"This is it then, huh?" Ellie mumbled.

"What is?" Marcus said, shooting her a sidelong glance.

"Our last stand," she replied bitterly.

The three grew quiet as they watched the Horde a half mile away set up makeshift camps from cars and other refuge found around them.

"Set guards all around us," Ellie said. "I'm going to have a chat with our guests." She slid down the ladder to the ground and disappeared inside the hotel.

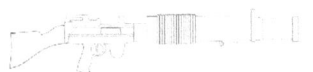

"So, you adapted to the dry heat? Is that why you're here?" Ellie said, slamming a fist into the bars. She ignored the pain that shot up her bones.

The creature stared up at her, a look of confusion plastered on its sickly green skin.

"Why are you here?" Ellie asked. "And don't lie to me."

"Lie?"

"Oh, now you don't understand?" Ellie growled. "Guards, get me the keys. Let's see if she understands the barrel of my pistol."

"No, no lie!" the creature said shrilly.

"Then why are you here?"

"Freedom!" it replied.

"Bullshit! Your friends out there don't seem to want freedom. They're looking to extinguish us!"

Confusion spread across its face again. "Friends out there?"

"Yes, your 'friends' are out there, surrounding us. Did you lead them here?"

"No! Scared!" it replied.

"You have me to be scared of; now tell me, why are you here?"

"Freedom! Please!"

Ellie pulled her pistol and clicked the hammer back. Although it didn't need to be cocked, the motion shocked anyone on the other end with the seriousness of the action. "If you say freedom one more time, I swear to god I'll end you."

"I help you. Please. I teach you," the creature said, shielding the smaller Horde creature as it began to cry in a shrill whimper.

The proposal of being taught anything snapped Ellie from her anger. The thought she had of her dad earlier in the council meeting was suddenly fresh in her mind. She felt as if a bucket of cold water had been thrown at her. She clicked the hammer down and holstered it. "Teach me? Teach me what?"

"Win friends," the creature said.

Ellie furrowed her brow. "What do you mean?"

"Human weak. Show strength. Be war chief. Win friends," the creature said.

"I don't understand," Ellie said.

"Horde here to find freedom from the old world. Earth is supposed to be empty. Old War Chief start a fight with humans. Start war. Show strength. Both sides stubborn, scared, protecting family," the creature said, pulling the other three in the cage closer. "Family, sacred."

"Can there ever be peace?" Ellie asked.

The creature shrugged. "Horde old, frail. Dying."

"We'll fight to the last man," Ellie whispered as she began to understand. "Until there is no one left."

"No family, no friends."

Ellie peered at her and nodded. "I want to know more about your world."

The creature approximated a smile, though its complexion and gnarled, misshapen teeth did not give it warmth. "No time. Must choose." The creature stood and walked over to the bars to face Ellie. "I choose family." It said, motioning to the three behind her.

Ellie glanced at them and then back into the dark green eyes of the creature. The thought of her dad once

78

again appeared in her mind's eye the last day she saw him. He had sacrificed himself for her. She understood now what the creature was asking. She wanted to sacrifice herself for the freedom of her children.

"Y-you want us to lead your people," Ellie said.

"No," the creature said, glancing at Ellie's pistol. "Want freedom."

"You want us to kill you," Ellie said with sudden realization. She backed up and stumbled over the chair.

"Freedom," the creature whispered harshly. "Tired, hungry, lost."

Ellie stared at the creature, her mouth agape. Taking the life of another soldier in the name of an ideal or for some preconceived notion of honor or duty was one thing. Asking to be summarily executed into extinction was another.

"Please."

"I-I can't."

"For peace."

Ellie peered at the Horde creatures in the cage. Her heart raced in her chest, its thunderous beat deafening in her ears. "No," she said, as her eyes caught the lifeless dolls in the corner. "I'm not a murderer; there is no need for them to die because of us."

The Horde nodded. "Give them freedom?"

"In a way, yes." She walked over to the guard and held out a hand for the keys. "Give me the keys, and report to the wall."

"Yes, of course," the guard said, handing her the requested item before disappearing up the stairs.

"Open the gate." She called. Confusion echoed across the wall, and she yelled louder. They did so with

79

reluctance. Ellie led the elder creature out into the streets beyond the wall, and they made their way toward the staging area of the Horde.

As she drew closer, a half dozen Horde from the opposing side began approaching, their high-tech rifles held in large, meaty hands. She could hear Marcus on the wall yelling for her to return, but she ignored him. Halfway to the Hordes' encampment, she stopped and waited for the small war party to approach.

"I kneel in front of you, make you look good. Show no fear," the captive said.

"I will do what I can for your younglings," Ellie whispered.

"No, have trust for us. Understand. You want peace. Show no mercy," the creature whispered.

"How will killing you four compel those brutes over there from killing me where I stand?"

"Family sacred."

Ellie's eyes widened. The creature nodded as the realization dawned on her.

"Family," the creature said, holding a hand to its chest.

"No, I can't. I'm... I'm not evil," Ellie said as she tried to swallow the lump in her throat. "There has to be a different way."

"This way, freedom. Peace."

"No," Ellie said softly as the Horde war party loomed before her. Ellie slid the pistol from its holster. She caressed the warn handle, her thoughts once again on her father. He never taught her how to deal with impossible choices. It was why she chose to rely on instinct. Now, she is faced with a moral decision that goes against her beliefs. She didn't know what to do.

The leader, a large Horde with dark green skin and black eyes, stopped a few yards away. He growled, howled, and grunted.

"He says release us, and your deaths will be swift."

"Tell him-" she stopped, looked at her prisoners, then glanced over her shoulder to the last stronghold of humanity. "Tell him he will go no further, and this ends here," she said as she leveled the pistol at the prisoner's head and clicked the hammer back.

The War Chief started forward but froze, clearly unsure of what to do. He responded with renewed growls and grunts.

"He demands, let the family go," the prisoner said. "Freedom."

"Tell him they are already dead," Ellie said as she raised a hand up. On her command, three wrapped bundles were tossed unceremoniously over the wall to the dirt. The War Chief howled in rage, and as he took a step, the prisoner glanced up at Ellie and said, "Thank y-"before being silenced by the thunder of a gunshot.

The War Chief froze mid-stride, falling to his knees as if the strings of his family were what held him up. His guards laid their weapons down and kneeled with bowed heads.

"It didn't have to be this way," Ellie said, tears streaking down her face. "God damn it." Ellie walked over to the War Chief and shot him point blank as if she were putting down a rabid dog. One by one, she saw the Horde further down the road lay their weapons down and kneel before her.

"God damn us all to hell," Ellie said as she pulled the trigger again.

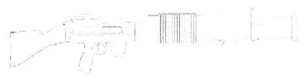

Her hand was sore from having to pull the trigger so many times. It grew heavier with each click and began to slump with her shoulders. Blood soaked her face. Some of the other soldiers from the city had joined her as they executed the remaining Horde. The streets of Sin City ran dark green with the blood of the Horde as the stench of it grew thick in the hot, oppressive air.

She walked through the gate and slumped down to her knees. Marcus ran over to her and slid down beside her. She pushed him away. She didn't want to feel anything other than self-loathing, disgust, and hatred for herself. She wanted nothing more than to end it all. Tears mingled with green blood that dripped down onto the sand.

The sunset, and still, she kneeled in the dirt and cried. Marcus knelt beside her, unsure how to comfort her. People mulled around, tending to various tasks, unaware of the sacrifice she had made for them. No one would ever know she had murdered an entire civilization. No one would ever know she had killed innocent creatures for them. It was the three smaller Horde creatures she worried the most about. Would they ever forgive her? She doubted it. She wouldn't. They would never know she had damned them all to hell in the name of freedom. For peace. The cost was forever hers to bear.

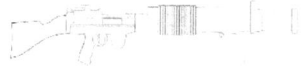

THANK YOU

As always, there are so many people that have helped me get here. I want to thank my wife and daughter for supporting me and helping me when I need it. Without them, I wouldn't have gotten this far. I want to thank my friends who continue to push me in being the best author I can be. Without them, I wouldn't have even started down this path. And of course, I want to thank you, the reader. Without you, I wouldn't be able to share these amazing stories. I hope you enjoy them as much as I enjoyed writing them and getting them out to you! I have plenty of more stories on the way. So, stay tuned for more!

Be sure to follow me!

Twitter: @youngantheretro

Facebook: @ddickinson

Website: http://www.tigerforce.net

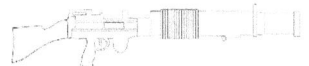

Order Gathering Tide today!

Order Don't Close Your Eyes today!